The Thread of Life

TWELVE OLD ITALIAN TALES

The Thread of Life

Retold by
DOMENICO VITTORINI

Illustrated by
MARY GRANDPRÉ

Running Press
KIDS
PHILADELPHIA • LONDON

Printed in China

Originally published in different form by David McKay
Company, Inc. in 1958 under the title *Old Italian Tales*.

Hand lettering and ink pen by Kara Fellows.

9   8   7   6   5   4   3   2   1
Digit on the right indicates the number of this printing

Library of Congress Cataloging-in-Publication Data is available for this title.

ISBN: 0-7624-1669-6

This book may be ordered by mail from the publisher.
Please include $2.50 for postage and handling.
But try your bookstore first!

Published by Running Press Kids,
an imprint of
Running Press Book Publishers
125 South Twenty-second Street
Philadelphia, Pennsylvania 19103-4399

Visit us on the web!
www.runningpress.com

For my la sorelle e il fratello,
Joan, Linda and Tom
M.G.

FOREWORD

*M*y sister, Helen, and I were privileged as children to be blessed with a remarkable father. Aside from his admirable profession as a teacher at the University of Pennsylvania, where he taught Romance languages and world literature, my father loved filling a room with laughter. Another love was sharing the simple retelling of Italian folktales—the folktales he had heard as a child and which were really the inspiration for his own life's work. What I mean to say is, what he loved most *was* his life's work. For me, this feeling permeates every page of this book.

I have wonderful boyhood memories of many evenings when my father would tell these tales to me. When he finished a story and I'd be going off to bed, he would say this gentle Italian expression: *"Dìo ti benedica."* These are words to be said to all children: "May God say good things to you" or "God bless you." These are words I still hear him say today!

As a teacher, my father sought to assist those who needed help with their studies. So Saturday mornings at our home were devoted to free tutoring for any and all who came for counsel, advice, and wisdom.

And so this reissue of my father's collection *Old Italian Tales* is dedicated not only to his memory but also to his daily presence in my life and in the lives of those students who were as vital to his pleasure in work as to his pleasure in life.

Carlo Vittorini,
New York City, 1995

CONTENTS

The Most Precious Possession

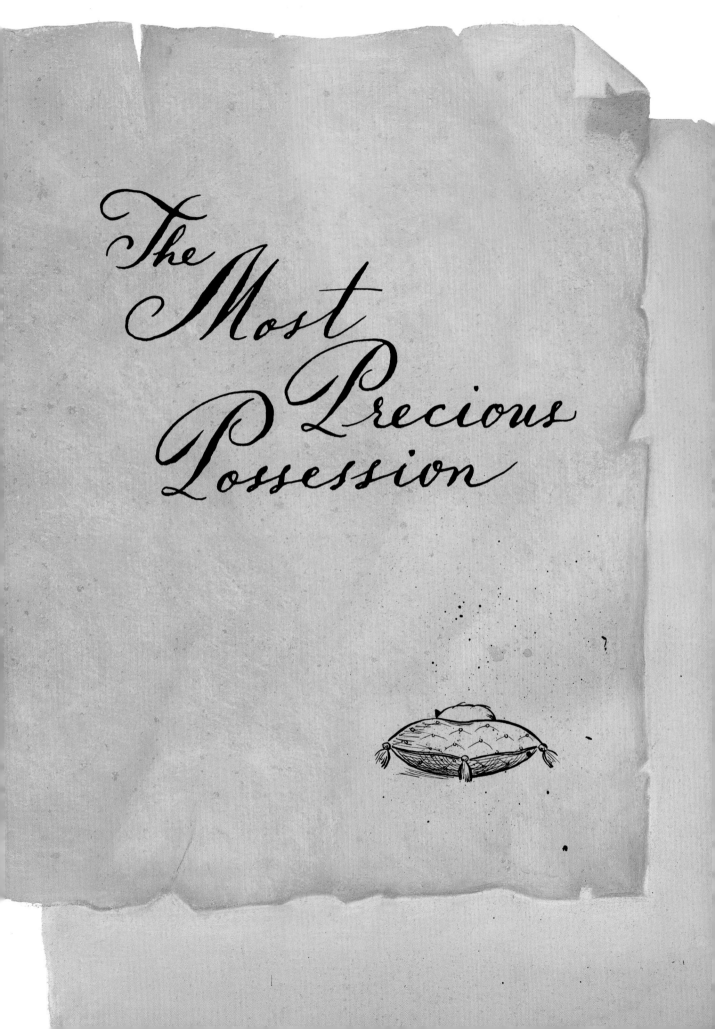

here was a time when Italian traders and explorers, finding the way to the East blocked by the Turks, turned west in their search for new lands to trade with—a search that led them to the New World.

In those days there lived in Florence a merchant by the name of Ansaldo. He belonged to the Ormanini family, known not only for its wealth but also for the daring and cunning of its young men. It happened that on one of his trips in search of adventure and trade, Ansaldo ventured beyond the Strait of Gibraltar and, after battling a furious storm, landed on one of the Canary Islands.

The king of the island welcomed him cordially, for the Florentines were well known to him. He ordered a magnificent banquet prepared and arranged to have it served in the sumptuous hall, resplendent with mirrors and gold, in which he had received Ansaldo.

When it was time to serve the meal, Ansaldo noticed with surprise that a small army of youths, carrying long stout sticks, entered and lined up against the walls of

the banquet hall. As each guest sat down, one of the youths took up a place directly behind him, the stick held in readiness to strike.

Ansaldo wondered what all this meant and wracked his brain for some clue to these odd goings-on. He didn't have long to wait. Suddenly a horde of huge ferocious rats poured into the hall and threw themselves upon the food that was being served. Pandemonium broke loose as the boys darted here and there, wielding the sticks.

For many years the Florentines had enjoyed the reputation of being the cleverest people on earth, able to cope with any situation. Ansaldo saw a chance to uphold the tradition. He asked the king's permission to go back to his ship, and returned shortly with two big Persian cats. These animals were much admired and loved by the Florentines and Venetians, who had first seen them in the East and who had brought many of them back to Italy. Ever since, one or two cats always completed the crew of a ship when it set out on a long journey.

Ansaldo let the cats go, and before long the entire hall was cleared of the revolting and destructive rats.

The astonished and delighted king thought he was witnessing a miracle. He could not find words enough to thank Ansaldo, whom he hailed as the savior of the island, and when Ansaldo made him a present of the cats, his gratitude knew no bounds.

After a pleasant visit, Ansaldo made ready to sail for home. The king accompanied him to his ship, and there he showered him with rich and rare gifts, much gold and silver, and many precious stones of all kinds and colors—rubies, topazes, and diamonds.

Ansaldo was overwhelmed not only by these costly gifts but also by the king's gratitude and the praises he heaped upon him and the cats. As for the latter, they were regarded with awe by all the islanders and as their greatest treasure by the king and the entire royal household.

When Ansaldo returned home, he regaled his friends with the account of his strange adventure. There was among them a certain Giocondo de Fifanti, who was as rich in envy as he was poor in intelligence. He thought, If the island king gave Ansaldo all these magnificent gifts for two mangy cats, what will he not give me if I present him with the most beautiful and precious things that our city of Florence has to offer?

No sooner said than done. He purchased lovely belts, necklaces, bracelets studded with diamonds, exquisite pictures, luxurious garments, and many other expensive gifts, and took ship for the now-famous Canary Islands.

After an uneventful crossing he arrived in port and hastened to the royal palace. He was received with more pomp than was Ansaldo. The king was greatly touched by the splendor of Giocondo's gifts and wanted to be equally generous. He held a long consultation with his people and then informed Giocondo happily that they had decided to let him share with his visitor their most precious possession. Giocondo could hardly contain his curiosity. However, the day of departure finally arrived and found Giocondo on his ship, impatiently awaiting the visit of the king. Before long the king, accompanied by the entire royal household and half the islanders, approached the ship. The king himself carried the precious gift on a silken cushion. With great pride he put the cushion into Giocondo's outstretched greedy hands. Giocondo was speechless. On the cushion, curled up in sleepy, furry balls, were two of the kittens that had been born to the Persian cats Ansaldo had left on the island.

The old story does not go on to say whether Giocondo, on his return to Florence, ever regaled his friends with the tale of *his* adventure!

A Wise Sentence

*I*n the city of Alexandria, which was built many hundreds of years ago by Alexander the Great, it was once customary to sell food in the streets, cooked right there in little portable kitchens. One morning Fabrac, a Saracen, was standing near his little kitchen when he noticed a poor man approach. The man had a hard piece of bread in his hand. He was so poor that he could not afford to buy anything at all to eat with his bread.

Fabrac was cooking a meat stew, and from the pot on his stove arose a delicate aroma. The poor man came closer. He sniffed the delicious aroma. Then he put out his arm and held the piece of bread in the fragrant steam, turning the crust this way and that until it was thoroughly saturated. Then eagerly he took a bite. Oh, how wonderful the bread tasted! The poor man ate it all up, to the last crumb.

For some reason Fabrac was in a very bad humor that morning. Perhaps business wasn't going well, or perhaps—but no matter the reason. The poor man's actions made Fabrac very angry. He seized the man by the arm and shouted, "You have taken something from me and you must pay for it."

"But I have taken nothing from you," replied the other. "I merely held a piece of bread in the steam from your pot."

Fabrac, angrier than ever, insisted, "The pot is mine and therefore its steam is mine, too. And so you must pay me for what is mine."

Of course the poor man couldn't pay Fabrac, but the latter raised such a hullabaloo that the matter came to the attention of the sultan.

"This is a most interesting state of affairs," said the sultan. He called together his court of wise men, presented the problem to them, and asked them to render a just decision.

The wise men began to quibble over the problem. Some took the part of the poor man. They said the steam did not belong to the stingy cook, for it did not have any real form and it did not change into food. Therefore, they concluded wisely, the poor man owed the cook nothing.

On the other hand, there were some who took the part of the cook. They claimed that the steam was connected with the meat, that the meat was unquestionably the property of the cook, and that therefore anything connected with the cook's property also belonged to him. Therefore, they also concluded wisely that not only custom but also law decreed that anyone who took something from someone else had to pay for it, and so they said the poor man did owe the cook for the steam.

The sultan listened attentively to both sides, his long beard in his hand, his head bowed in deep thought. After a while he raised his head and in a voice of authority said, "There is no doubt but that the poor man has taken something that was related to what the cook was selling. But there is the same relation between the meat and the steam as there is between a coin and the sound it makes. Let the poor man, therefore, flip a coin on the counter of the cook's kitchen, and let the cook consider himself paid with the sound of the coin for the steam of his meat."

And so the sultan solved this most unusual problem.

The One-Legged Crane

ome people, finding themselves in a tight spot, feel completely helpless, caught like a mouse in a trap. But others, with a ready wit and a quick tongue, call these blessings to their aid and lose no time in freeing themselves from their difficulties. There are many amusing stories about such nimble-witted ones. One of the best is about a cook, and although it is hundreds of years old, the story can still make us chuckle. And here it is.

There once lived in the city of Florence a very handsome and pleasure-loving prince called Corrado. Corrado loved to go hunting, and after each hunt he loved to entertain his guests at a great banquet. Not only Corrado's lavish table, but also the way the dishes were brought to it made him the talk of Florence. And what was the secret of the prince's unusual entertainment? I'll tell you. It was his cook.

Yes, Corrado had a marvelous cook who went by the strange name of Chichibio. But make no mistake about it. Chichibio was not just a cook. He was a kitchen poet, a culinary artist. Chichibio was never content merely to roast a wild boar, a partridge, or a pheasant and to serve it in the customary way. Oh, no. Chichibio would create the game's natural setting on a huge platter, set the animal or fowl on it, surrounded by the miniature trees and plants, carry it proudly into the vast banquet hall, and finally place it on the long banquet table, enjoying to the full the cries of surprise and delight that greeted him. Sometimes the guests even clapped their hands and shouted "Bravo! Bravo!" Chichibio would accept their applause and praise with a modest bow while his master looked fondly on. The prince was very proud of Chichibio and considered himself extremely lucky to have such a talented cook.

Chichibio was not much to look at. His features were coarse and heavy, and he held his head a little to one side. No one would guess that he was a clever and quick-witted man as well as

an excellent

cook. But the twinkle in his eye belied the seeming dullness of his appearance, and those who knew him were aware of how shrewd he really was and what a genius he had for getting out of trouble.

Now listen to what happened one day and decide for yourself whether or not this was true.

On this particular day Corrado went hunting with his favorite falcon and caught a young and beautiful crane. Cranes were a rare delicacy, so Corrado looked forward with pleasure to the banquet he planned for his guests that night. As soon as he returned from the hunt, he called Chichibio to him, gave him the crane, and ordered him to prepare it in the most novel way he knew. Promising to outdo himself to please his master, Chichibio went back to the kitchen and set to work. As he plucked the crane and cleaned it and stuffed it, flavoring it with many fine herbs and spices brought to Italy from the Orient by the seafaring Venetian traders, Chichibio wracked his brain for an unusual idea. He wanted to present the crane as no crane had ever been presented before. Finally the crane was set to roast on the spit. Soon such a delicious aroma filled the kitchen that Chichibio thought it was powerful enough to bring a dead man back to life.

Well, the aroma didn't quite do *that*, but it did bring to the kitchen door Brunetta, the pretty village girl with whom Chichibio was very much in love.

"Oh, Chichibio," cried Brunetta, "what *is* that heavenly smell? I was passing by and just had to stop. It absolutely drew me here."

Chichibio took her into the kitchen and showed her the crane, roasting on the spit and sending out with every turn the most marvelous fragrance. Brunetta's mouth began to water. She came as close to the open fire as she dared. Pointing her finger at the fowl, she said, "I simply must have a leg of that crane."

Chichibio thought she was joking. He wagged his finger under her pert little nose and playfully chanted, "You shall not have it from me. You shall not have it from me." But Brunetta was not joking at all. The delicious aroma was more than she could bear. Annoyed with Chichibio, she turned angrily on her heel, muttered "All right, if you care more about an old crane than about me," and started to leave the kitchen. The thought of losing Brunetta was more than Chichibio could bear, so he reached over, hastily tore off one of the crane's legs, and gave it to the girl. All smiles now, Brunetta snatched the crane's leg and greedily began to eat it.

Poor Chichibio! How could he serve a one-legged crane without anyone detecting the deception? He thought and thought, and at last an idea came to him. He remembered that cranes, when asleep, stood on one leg. Chichibio decided to serve up a sleeping crane at the banquet that night.

And so he did. Before the astonished guests Chichibio set down a tremendous platter. Reeds and rushes had made of it a forest glade in the midst of which stood the crane on one leg, fast asleep. Corrado and all the guests burst into spontaneous applause. However, it did not take the prince long to discover that the crane had but one leg. He turned to Chichibio and demanded to know what had become of the other leg.

Chichibio feigned surprise. Opening his eyes very wide, he said, "The other leg? What other leg? Why, I always thought that cranes had only one leg."

Corrado did not wish to make a scene in front of his guests, so he only said, "Indeed? We'll see about that in the morning."

At dawn the next day the prince ordered Chichibio to mount up and accompany him in a search for some cranes. "I'd like you to prove to me that they have only one leg," he told his cook.

They had not gone very far when they came upon a beautiful shady meadow with a lovely stream. It was an ideal spot for cranes to spend the night. As Corrado

and Chichibio entered the glade, they saw several cranes in the stream, still asleep, and standing on one leg.

Chichibio, who had been shaking in his boots all the way, now drew a sigh of relief. "You can readily see, my lord," he said, "that I spoke the truth last night."

Too angry to answer, Corrado spurred his horse, rushed toward the cranes, and shouted "Ho! Ho!" at the top of his lungs.

Startled, as was to be expected, the cranes put down their other leg and rose in sudden flight. Corrado galloped back to the quaking cook and demanded furiously, "How many legs do cranes have, Chichibio?"

"Two, my lord," Chichibio replied humbly. "I must have been mistaken."

"Then, Chichibio," thundered the prince, "where was our crane's other leg last night?"

Frightened as he was, Chichibio did not lose his wits. He looked up at his master and said with an air of injured innocence, "Oh, but last night, my lord, you did not shout 'Ho! Ho!' to the crane. If you had, it would most certainly have put down its other leg."

In spite of his anger, Corrado was so amused by Chichibio's answer that he burst into laughter and forgave his clever cook.

March
and the
Shepherd

One morning at the very beginning of spring, a shepherd led his sheep to graze, and on the way he met March.

"Good morning," said March. "Where are you going to take your sheep to graze today?"

"Well, March, today I am going to the mountains."

"Fine, Shepherd. That's a good idea. Good luck." But to himself March said, "Here's where I have some fun, for today I'm going to fix you."

And that day in the mountains the rain came down in buckets. It was a veritable deluge. The shepherd, however, had watched March's face very carefully and noticed a mischievous look on it. So instead of going to the mountains, he had remained in the plains. In the evening, upon returning home, he met March again.

"Well, Shepherd, how did it go today?"

"It couldn't have been better. I changed my mind and went to the plains. A very beautiful day. Such a lovely warm sun."

"Really? I'm glad to hear it," said March, but he bit his lip in vexation. "Where are you going tomorrow?"

"Tomorrow I'm going to the plains, too. With this fine weather, I would be crazy if I went to the mountains."

"Oh, really? Fine! Farewell."

And they parted.

But the shepherd didn't go to the plains again. He went to the mountains. And on the plains March brought rain and wind and hail—a punishment indeed from heaven. In the evening he met the shepherd homeward bound.

"Good evening, Shepherd. How did it go today?"

"Very well indeed. Do you know? I changed my mind again and went to the mountains after all. It was heavenly there. What a day! What a sky! What a sun!"

"I'm really happy to hear it, Shepherd. And where are you going tomorrow?"

"Well, tomorrow I'm going to the plains. I see dark clouds over the mountains. I wouldn't want to find myself too far from home."

To make a long story short, whenever the shepherd met March, he always told him the opposite of what he planned to do the next day, so March was never able to catch him. The end of the month came, and on the last day, the thirtieth, March said to the shepherd, "Well, Shepherd, how is everything?"

"Things couldn't be any better. This is the end of the month and I'm out of danger. There's nothing to fear now. I can begin to sleep peacefully."

"That's true," said March. "And where are you going tomorrow?"

The shepherd, certain that he had nothing

to fear, told March the truth.
"Tomorrow," he said, "I shall go to
the plains. The distance is shorter
and the work less hard."

"Fine. Farewell."

March hastened to the home of his cousin April and
told her the whole story. "I want you to lend me at least one day," he
said. "I am determined to catch this shepherd." Gentle April was unwilling
but March coaxed so hard that finally she consented.

The following morning the shepherd set off for the plains. No sooner had his
flock scattered than there arose a storm that
chilled his very heart. The sharp wind
howled and growled, snow fell in

thick, icy flakes, hail pelted down. It was all the shepherd could do to get his sheep back into the fold.

That evening as the shepherd huddled in a corner of his hearth, silent and melancholy, March paid him a visit.

"Good evening, Shepherd," he said.

"Good evening, March."

"How did it go today?"

"I'd rather not talk about it," said the shepherd. "I can't understand what happened. Not even in the middle of January have I ever seen a storm like the one on the plains today. It seemed as if all the devils had broken loose from hell. Today I had enough rough weather to last me the whole year. And oh, my poor sheep!"

Then at last was March satisfied.

And from that time on March has had thirty-one days because, as it is said in Tuscany, the rascal never returned to April the day he borrowed from her.

The Three Fools

*B*astianello was a young man of good peasant stock. He was keen-minded, practical, and hardworking, and when he reached his twenty-fifth year, he decided to get married. He cast his eye on Rosetta, a nice, quiet, healthy girl of the neighborhood. Like the good son that he was, Bastianello went to his parents and told them of his intentions, and they went to the mother and father of Rosetta. Both families were delighted, so the wedding took place after a few months of courtship.

The wedding dinner was drawing to a close when Bastianello noticed that the wine was almost gone and called for more. The bride, to show what a dutiful wife she would make, offered to fetch it, and down she went to the wine cellar with a huge pitcher in her hand, while all the jovial guests applauded approvingly.

Rosetta sat down on a small stool, placed the pitcher under a large cask of wine, and opened the tap. The wine flowed into the pitcher as red as a ruby, and Rosetta, her elbows resting on her knees, her hands propped under her red cheeks, began to think.

Let us imagine, she told herself, that in time I will have a baby and that I will call him Bastianello after his father and that suddenly he will die. What will I do? She burst into uncontrollable sobbing and weeping while the wine overflowed the pitcher and began to spread over the floor.

Rosetta's mother-in-law, seeing that the bride did not return, hastened down to the cellar. Upon hearing the reason for the girl's tears, she too began to wail. And the wine continued to spread over the cellar floor.

Above, the men grew thirstier and thirstier and called loudly for the return of the women with more wine. The father-in-law, greatly concerned, hurried down to the cellar and he too, informed of the sad thought that had come to Rosetta, joined the women. So the three sat there and cried and sobbed with all their hearts. They were a sight to behold. And the wine kept on flowing, flooding the cellar.

Bastianello, worried beyond measure, finally ran down to the cellar. First, seeing all the wine going to waste, he hastened to turn off the tap. Then he inquired of his bride and his parents what terrible thing had befallen them to cause them to weep so brokenheartedly. When he heard the reason for their lamentations, he flew into a rage and shouted, "Imbeciles! Is it possible that there can be such idiots in the world? To think such far-fetched nonsense and sit and sob over it while the good wine goes to waste!

it never be said that Bastianello will spend his life with fools. I'll go wandering all over the world and I won't return until I find three persons more foolish than you." And he stormed out of the house.

That very afternoon Bastianello came upon a man near a well. He was drenched with water and perspiration and looked most disconsolate.

"Whatever are you doing, my friend?" asked Bastianello.

"I'm trying to fill a large pail with water," answered the man, "but I do not seem to be getting anywhere, and I don't know why."

Bastianello investigated the matter and saw that the man was using a sieve to carry the water from the well to the pail.

"Why don't you use a regular bucket instead of a sieve full of holes?" Bastianello asked.

"That's a good idea!" exclaimed the poor man. "I hadn't thought of it."

Bastianello shook his head and said to himself, "Here is one more stupid than my family."

At dusk, as he was passing along a country road, Bastianello noticed a man in his underwear climbing a tree from which he tried to jump into a pair of trousers that his wife was holding out for him. Each time, as he made the leap, the heavy feet of the peasant knocked the trousers from the hands of his spouse. Tired and bewildered, the man climbed the tree again and again and tried to jump into the trousers, only to knock them, each time, out of the hands of his wife.

Bastianello watched this strange performance for a while and then asked, "What on earth are you trying to do?"

The man explained that he was merely trying to put on his trousers.

"Fool!" cried Bastianello impatiently. "Why don't you just lean against the tree, hold your trousers so, and pull them up?"

The man looked at Bastianello in great surprise. "What a wonderful idea!" he exclaimed, clapping his hand to his forehead. "I would never have thought of it. Thank you, thank you, my friend."

Bastianello shook his head and said to himself, "Here is another more foolish than my family."

Later that same night Bastianello reached the gates of a town not far from his own village. He noticed with surprise a large crowd attending a wedding party. The members were all on horseback. A difficulty had arisen because the gateway was too low for the tall bride to enter on her big horse. An excited discussion was going on between the bridegroom and the owner of the horse. Apparently it had been suggested that the only thing to do was either to cut off the head of the bride or the hoofs of the horse. The bridegroom was defending the head of his beloved with passion and vehemence, and the owner of the horse, with equal vehemence and passion, was defending the hoofs of his horse.

Bastianello stepped between them and said, "My friends, permit me. I'll solve your problem."

He drew near the horse and lightly kicked it, at the same time gently pushing down the bride's head. Thus she was able to enter the gateway. All looked at Bastianello as if he were a great genius while he shook his head over their stupidity.

Realizing that the world was full of fools and seeing that in one day he was able to find three persons more idiotic than his wife and his parents, Bastianello decided not to go wandering but to return home and make the best of things. So he went back and he was welcomed with open arms by his loving wife and proud parents.

The Man, the Serpent, and the Fox

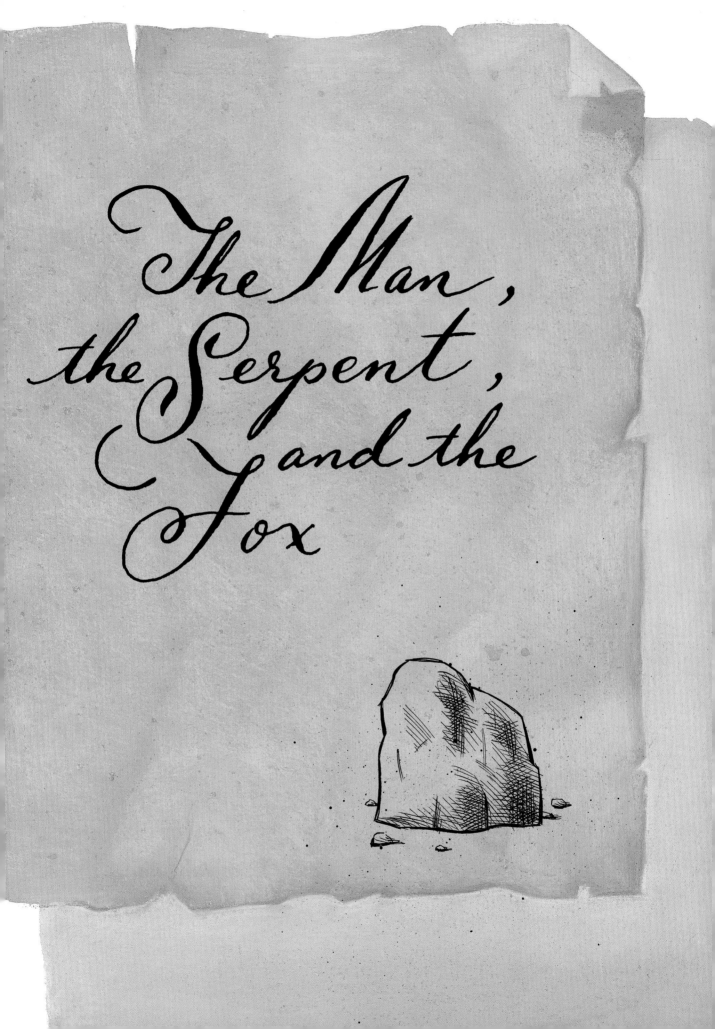

*O*nce upon a time a hunter passed through a quarry and saw a serpent caught under an enormous rock. The serpent begged the hunter to free him, but the man said, "No, I won't, for if I do, you will surely bite me."

The serpent replied, "Free me, and I promise not to bite you."

When the man had freed the serpent, it suddenly turned on him and tried to devour him. In vain the man backed away, crying, "You ungrateful thing! Did you not promise not to bite me?"

The serpent, still pursuing him, said, "Hunger knows no promises, my friend."

Seeing himself lost, the man, still walking backward, begged the serpent to give him a chance. "Let us ask three animals whether or not you have the right to devour me," he said. "If they all say yes, you may eat me up. If even one says no, you must not touch me."

The serpent agreed, and they set out in search of the three judges. The first one they met was a mangy old greyhound, so weak he could barely drag himself along. They asked him if the serpent had the right to eat his benefactor.

With bitterness and hatred in his voice, the greyhound answered, "I once had a master. Together we hunted every kind of game—hares, partridges, quail, and pheasant. He was very happy with me and petted me and gave me the best that he had to eat. But now that I am old and too tired to hunt, he has chased me out of his house and wants to kill me. That is Humankind for you. Go ahead and devour this one, Serpent! Make him pay for the injustices that Humankind inflicts on us beasts."

"Do you hear?" exclaimed the serpent. "This judge is in perfect agreement with me."

The hunter said nothing, and they continued on their way. The second animal they met was an old horse who was nothing but skin and bones.

The same question was put to him, and he said, "The serpent has every right to eat up the man. My master is planning to kill me after I have worked for him and served him faithfully all my life. Go ahead, Serpent. Bite, and eat up the most ungrateful beast in the world—Man."

The serpent licked his lips with his forked tongue and said with a flash of desire in his eyes, "Did you hear that? This judge too is on my side."

The hunter was thoroughly frightened now but continued on the way with the serpent. The third animal they met was a fox to whom they put the same question. But the fox did not answer at once in a simple and straightforward way. He assumed the thoughtful air of a judge. He looked severely first at the man, then at the serpent.

At last he gravely said, "Before I can come to a just decision, I must know with absolute precision all the details, even the slightest, of what has taken place. Let us return to the quarry. You, Serpent, in my presence, put yourself again under the rock. And you, Man, will then proceed to free him. Then I shall be in a position to pronounce my sentence."

This is precisely what they did. The foolish serpent placed himself again under the rock, and the man made sure he was held fast.

"Are you under the rock?" The fox sneered, "Good. And there, ungrateful creature who does not keep his promise, there you shall remain forever."

And that is why, even today, serpents are found under rocks.

A Strange Reward

$\mathcal{J}$n days gone by there was a king in France named Philip of Valois. He loved to wear beautiful clothes and to entertain lavishly, but most of all he loved to go hunting. In those days falcons were used to catch small game. In every royal court there were many skillful falconers whose duty it was to train these birds of prey and to accompany the king in the hunt. The falcon perched on the clenched fist of the falconer, its head covered with a small hood. When the game was sighted, the hood was removed and the falcon sought the game, which it retrieved, much in the manner of a bird dog today.

Philip had a favorite falcon, strong, swift, and beautiful. He loved it very much, and as a sign of his favor he had hung on its neck a necklace of gold and silver bells engraved with the lilies of his coat of arms.

One day the king went hunting with his beloved falcon. They spotted a partridge, and the falcon caught it and brought it back to the king. Then they sighted another partridge and the falcon was set to pursue it. But, having caught it, the bird flew away with it, much to the chagrin of the king and the falconers.

Philip sent eight of his best men to find the falcon, but in vain. The bird had returned to the freedom of the forest and the open air. The king was much saddened by his loss. He offered two hundred ducats to anyone who brought back his beautiful falcon. The news of the reward spread quickly to every corner of the kingdom.

One day a peasant working in his field heard the tinkle of bells. He looked up and to his astonishment saw in a nearby tree a falcon wearing a necklace of gold and silver bells. He knew at once that it was the king's falcon. The peasant stretched out his callused hand and coaxed the bird to come to him. The falcon was quite tame and used to men, so after hesitating a moment, it perched on the peasant's hand, much to the latter's joy.

The peasant had two daughters of marriageable age, but they could not find good husbands because they had no dowry. The peasant was a poor man, and besides, the harvest this year had been an unusually bad one. The question of providing his daughters with a dowry weighed heavily on the father's mind. But now, he realized happily, there might be an answer to his dilemma. Thinking of the reward, he was sure his daughters would now be able to find good husbands.

The peasant wasted no time. He left his hoe in the field, tied the falcon with a piece of rope that he had removed from his donkey's saddle, and off he went to the king's court. He arrived in due time and asked to see the king, but the guards laughed at him.

"Oh yes, the king has nothing better to do than to waste his time on any and every ragged peasant who comes up to the palace," they jeered. "Now move along, and be quick about it!"

But the peasant would not leave. He showed them the falcon and mentioned the reward the king had offered for its return.

"A likely story," mocked the guards. "Do you know how many people have already come here with falcons supposed to be the falcon of the king and mentioning the reward? How do we know this is the right one? Move along now."

But the peasant insisted, so finally the exasperated guards called one of the king's ministers. The minister was fat and pompous. He had full red cheeks, and he was dressed as gaudily as a peacock.

He listened to the peasant, examined the falcon and the bells carefully, and then said, "Yes, this is the king's falcon. But you don't even know how to hold it or how to treat it. Here, give it to me and I'll take it to the king."

"Perhaps I don't know how to hold it," said the peasant humbly, "but I beg you not to take away from me what fortune has given me. Let me take the falcon to the king. I'll carry it the best way I know."

The minister tried every trick he knew. He even tried threats, but the peasant held firm. Finally the minister said, "Oh, well, if you insist. But let's make a pact. Since I have a great deal of influence with the king, I'll put in a good word for you, and you must agree to give me half of whatever the king gives you."

The peasant understood exactly what the wily minister was up to, but he could see no way out and figured that half the reward would be better than no reward at all. So he agreed, and the minister obtained for him an audience with the king. Philip was overjoyed to see his falcon again. "Ask anything you wish," he told the peasant, and was greatly surprised when the peasant said, "This falcon came to me as God willed, and I have brought it back to you as best as I knew how. The reward I want is that you order your servant to give me fifty lashes with the whip."

Hearing this, the minister turned so pale he looked just like a ghost. The king marveled, and asked the reason for so strange a wish. The peasant then told him how the minister had forced him to promise to share with him half of whatever the king gave him, adding, "Your Majesty, I am a poor man, and I have two daughters for whom I must provide a dowry. But gladly will I forgo the reward that means the happiness of my children, and gladly will I endure my share of the whipping, and contented will I leave your presence if I can see this wicked man punished as he deserves."

The king, a wise man, sympathized fully with the feelings of the peasant and decided it would be only simple justice to grant his request. So one of his servants administered twenty-five lashes on the naked and fat back of the unworthy minister. When the turn came for the peasant to receive his lashes, the king said, "I have given you half the reward you asked, and thus you have kept your promise. Now, by virtue of my royal power, it is my pleasure to change the rest of the reward into the two hundred ducats I offered to the man who would bring back my falcon."

The peasant took the money and returned joyfully home. To each daughter he gave a handsome dowry of a hundred ducats, and soon after the girls became betrothed to two of the best-looking young men in the village.

Cenerentola

*O*nce upon a time there was a man who had three daughters. All his tenderness and affection were for the two older ones, and the youngest was left to attend to the menial work of the household. Since she was busy all day long working in the kitchen and sweeping the cinders on the hearth, she was called Cenerentola.

One day the father had to leave the city on business. He asked his daughters what they wanted him to bring back to them.

The oldest said, "A beautiful dress." The next daughter cried, "A lovely hat and a splendid shawl."

But when Cenerentola was asked what she wanted, she replied with her usual simplicity and modesty, "I should like to have the tiny bird called Verdeliò."

There was no way to make her change her mind, so the father set out on his trip and eventually returned with the gifts for his daughters.

It happened that the father was connected with the king's court. Shortly afterward, the king announced that he was going to give a magnificent ball and told the father it would make him happy to have his daughters among the guests. When the father returned home with this wonderful news, the two older girls began to tease Cenerentola unmercifully.

"What will you wear to the ball?" they cried. "What good is your Verdeliò to you now? You had better stay at home."

The evening of the ball arrived, and the two older sisters departed for the

festivities dressed like two princesses. Poor Cenerentola was left behind, sitting forlornly by the fire, polishing the copper pans.

But as soon as her sisters drove away, Cenerentola hastened to Verdeliò and said, "My little bird, please make me as beautiful as the sun." And there she stood, in an instant, dazzlingly beautiful and dressed in an exquisite sea-green gown glittering with diamonds. The bird gave her two purses full of golden coins and told her that a splendid coach was waiting outside to take her to the ball.

As soon as Cenerentola entered the great hall of the palace, all eyes turned toward her. The prince went to her at once and asked her to dance. He danced only

with her the entire evening, until the stroke of midnight, when the mysterious beauty made a curtsy to His Majesty the king and left the hall, followed by the admiring glances of everyone there. Passing by her sisters, she took out from one of her purses a tiny lace handkerchief, exquisitely embroidered, and a bracelet fell on the floor. The oldest sister picked it up and said, "Madam, this bracelet has fallen from your purse."

"Do keep it," answered the mysterious maiden in a sweet voice that sounded strangely familiar to the oldest sister.

The king had given strict orders to his servants to follow the coach of the mysterious maiden to see where she lived. As soon as her fiery steeds started, the servants followed on horseback. The girl took the golden coins and threw them out. While the servants stopped to pick them up, she disappeared.

When the sisters returned from the ball full of tales of their conquests and victories, Cenerentola was already in bed, humble as before.

On the following evening there was another ball at the palace and the two sisters attended again, as haughty and proud as usual. Soon after their arrival, the unknown maiden entered. She was more beautiful than ever. The light of her loveliness dazzled all who beheld her, and the young prince fell madly in love with her. However, he was no more successful this evening than he had been the one before in discovering who she was. At the stroke of midnight the mysterious visitor left the ball and the king's servants again followed her. When they had gone along part of the way, Cenerentola threw out handfuls of sand which so blinded the pursuers that they had to stop to wipe their faces, and while they were so engaged the coach and its mysterious occupant vanished.

The king then announced that another ball would be held on the third evening. As before, the sisters went off, decked out in satin and silk, and as before, no sooner had they left than Cenerentola said to her bird, "Little Verdelió of mine, this time make me more beautiful than ever." And she appeared at the ball as though dressed in heavenly hues, her gown sparkling with diamonds and precious stones, and her eyes shining like stars.

Again the prince danced with her alone, completely dazzled by her beauty and charm and modest manner. And again, promptly at the stroke of midnight she left, with the king's servants following her. But this time Cenerentola became a little confused because she realized she had nothing to throw back at her pursuers. In her haste to get away from them she lost one of her tiny slippers. The servants picked it up, hastened after the fleeing girl, and followed her coach to her very door.

The next day messengers and heralds from the king arrived at Cenerentola's house, the tiny slipper in their hands.

"Have you any daughters?" they asked the father.

"Yes," he answered. "I have—er—two."

Both daughters appeared and the slipper was tried on each, but it did not fit either of them.

The chief herald refused to believe that he was mistaken about seeing the fleeing girl stop at this house. He persisted in his search and then inquired of the father, "Is it really true that you do not have another daughter? Take care how you reply, for if you do not speak the truth your head will be the forfeit."

Then the older sisters became frightened and pretended just to have remembered something. "Oh, yes," they said, "we have a little sister, but she is such a cinder maid that we often forget all about her." And the father called hastily, "Cenerentola! Cenerentola! Where are you? Come quickly."

"Here I am, Father," Cenerentola answered, and appeared before them. But behold! This was no cinder maid. This was the lovely mysterious stranger who had so charmed everyone at each of the balls. She was dressed in the heavenly gown she had worn the night before, and her eyes shone like stars.

The chief herald knelt down and tried the tiny slipper on her foot. It fit perfectly. Then he bade her enter the royal coach, and they drove off to the court, leaving the father and sisters standing there with their mouths open in astonishment.

Need we add that the story ends happily? Cenerentola, so good and beautiful and modest, was married to the prince, and in time she became a kind and gentle queen.

The Adventurous Winnower

$\mathcal{I}$n the green and peaceful valleys of Tuscany, it used to be the custom for winnowers to go from town to town and from farm to farm during the harvest season, offering their services in helping to separate the chaff from the wheat. The winnower had to carry a large sieve over his shoulder and a heavy tripod from which hung three stout ropes. These held the sieve in place when it was being used. Upon reaching a farm, the winnower set up his tripod and, with a circular motion, shook the grain through the suspended sieve, thus causing the chaff to separate from the wheat. The work was tedious and tiresome, but even worse, it raised a constant cloud of thick dust that caused the winnower's eyes to smart and burn. Yes, the lot of these workers was difficult indeed.

Among these winnowers there was one called Parcittadino. Parcittadino grew tired of his wearisome trade and decided to become a court entertainer. He had a ready wit and was known as much for his gay tales as for his skill in his trade. So he said to himself, "Why not try my luck at the court of King Edward of England? His fame and liberality are known the world over, even here in Tuscany."

One morning, therefore, he set out for England. After several months on the road traveling by foot, and some weeks at sea, he reached the palace of the English king. He waited until the changing of the guards, and then he quietly slipped in. After passing through a long succession of rooms, he reached a hall where he found King Edward playing chess with his prime minister.

Parcittadino fell on his knees beside the king, but Edward was absorbed in the chessboard and gave no sign of having noticed him. Presently Parcittadino got up and began to speak in a soft voice:

"Blessed be the hour and the moment in which I arrived here where I have always longed to be. For I see the most noble, prudent, and valorous king in the world. I can truly boast now over my peers, for have I not seen the flower of royalty? How much glory my good luck has granted me! If I were to die at this very moment, gladly would I do so, for my eyes have seen the most royal crown that attracts men just as a magnet attracts metal."

Parcittadino had hardly finished this speech when the king, annoyed at being disturbed in his game by the lengthy praises of Parcittadino, rose from the chessboard, seized him, threw him down on the floor, and proceeded to give the poor winnower a sound beating. Having done this, the king returned to his game of chess, without saying one word.

Parcittadino painfully got to his feet. Although his bruises hurt him very much (for the king wielded a strong arm), he was hurt more by the thought that his long and arduous trip and his praises had come to such a sad end. He could not understand why King Edward had given him blows in return for the beautiful words he had spoken. Suddenly a brilliant idea flashed through his mind, and he thought, If this great king is accustomed to giving blows for praise, perhaps he gives gifts for insults.

Taking courage, he began a new speech, similar to the previous one but changing praise into harsh and violent accusations.

In a strong voice that echoed ominously through the great hall, he cried, "Cursed be the hour and the day in which I arrived here. I believed that I would see a king as noble as fame declares him to be. And what have I found? An ungrateful and vengeful king. I believed I would see a virtuous and generous king. But I found one vicious and miserly. I believed I would see a kind and sincere king. But I found one full of malice and iniquity."

Parcittadino would have continued this harangue, but the king rose again from the chessboard and, stepping to the door, called one of his attendants. The poor winnower trembled like a leaf and already considered himself a goner. No doubt the king would order the attendant to take Parcittadino off to the Tower of London. Instead, to the amazement of the winnower, the king ordered the attendant to fetch him the most beautiful mantle in his wardrobe, one made of pure silk, with mother-of-pearl buttons and embroidered with precious stones.

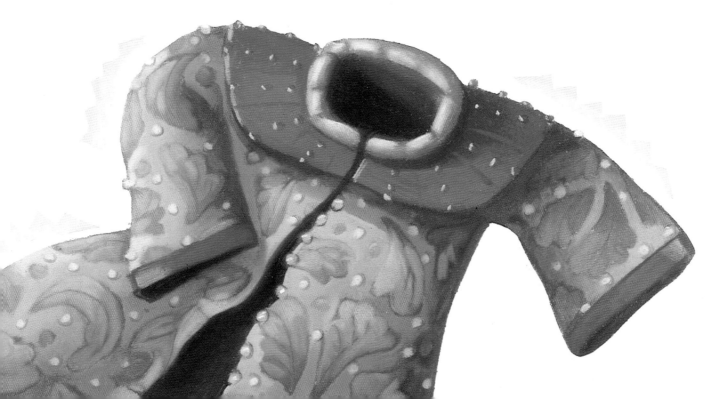

"Give the mantle to this man to pay him for the truths he has just revealed to me," the king said. "For his lies I have already paid him in full myself."

The confused Parcittadino couldn't believe his ears. He put on the magnificent robe. At first timidly, then regaining his assurance, he spoke up boldly. "If this is the way I am to be paid for my lies, seldom shall I speak the truth."

The king was pleased by these witty words and kept Parcittadino as court entertainer in his palace as long as he wished to stay. Several years went by and Parcittadino requested permission to leave England, for he longed for his beloved Tuscany. Back in Italy, he went from one nobleman's court to another relating his strange adventure, which so entertained his listeners that many a florin found its way into his pockets. Rich but weary, he at last reached his own little hometown. Here he found the people as poor as ever. Parcittadino shared his wealth with them. For the rest of his life he continued to make journeys in search of adventure, and never again did he take up the hard lot of the winnower.

The Wooden Bowl

*O*nce upon a time in far-off Italy there was a little boy whose name was Robertino and who loved his grandfather very much. The little boy and the old man were great friends and spent much time together. Robertino loved to sit at his grandfather's knee and listen, his gray eyes wide open, to the stories that he told him. Grandfather was a wonderful storyteller. And oh, the tales he told! Fairy tales and hero tales and exciting hunting stories, like the one in which Grandfather himself had once caught an eagle. Often Robertino and his grandfather would journey together to the land of make-believe to hunt imaginary lions and tigers. No matter how fantastic the stories or the games they played, the tie between these two was real enough, the only tie that kept the old man attached to this life.

Grandfather had come to live with Robertino's parents when Grandmother had died, three years before. Robertino's mother was a capable woman who took good care of her husband and her little son, but she did not understand the loneliness of the old man. Sometimes she was very impatient with him, especially these days when his hands trembled and every so often he would drop what he was holding in them.

One night after supper Grandfather picked up his cup to drink his coffee, but his poor old hands shook so that the coffee spilled on the clean white tablecloth, and the cup, falling from his hands, shattered into many pieces on the floor. Robertino's mother was angry and spoke harshly to the old man. Grandfather never said a word in reply, but only looked at her with hurt in his eyes. Robertino did not say anything either, but he couldn't eat any more supper, for his heart seemed ready to burst with sadness. Poor and dear Grandfather!

After that, Grandfather had to eat all by himself at a little table in the kitchen. He did not say anything when he was told about this new arrangement, but there was sadness in his eyes, and sadness in the gentle smile he gave his grandchild.

From that evening on, as soon as Robertino finished his supper, he would ask to be excused and he would run into the kitchen to be with the old man he loved so much. Grandfather would take him on his knee and begin a story, and as the magic words began to weave their spell, the bare little kitchen became a beautiful land where there was no pain and no sadness and where an old man and a little boy could roam happily hand in hand.

As time went on and Grandfather grew older, he became weaker and his hands shook more and more. One night as he sat all alone in the kitchen, his hands trembled so that he dropped his bowl of porridge. The porridge spilled all over the kitchen floor, and the bowl broke into many pieces. Robertino's father and mother, followed by the child, left the dining room where they had been eating and hastened to the kitchen. As they reached the door they saw the spilled porridge on the spotless floor.

Robertino was very much upset, not only by the indignation of his parents, but especially by the consternation of his grandfather. The old man was confused and crushed. Robertino's mother spoke more harshly than she had ever done before, scolded, and said the only thing to do was to give the old man a wooden bowl. She could not, she said, have her dishes broken just because he was so careless. She made a big fuss over cleaning up the floor. Robertino stood silently by as she mopped and polished until it was spotless again, scolding and mumbling resentfully all the while.

Suddenly the child went over to the fireplace, where his mother had swept the fragments of the bowl. He picked the pieces out carefully and began to put them together. He worked so earnestly that soon the bowl seemed to be whole. Then he took from the side of the hearth a small piece of wood and began to

whittle it, keeping his eyes on the earthen bowl as though it were a model. After a while his parents, curious to see what he was doing, went over to him.

"What are you making, Robertino?" asked his mother fondly. She always spoke kindly to her little son.

"I'm making a wooden bowl for you to have when you grow old," answered Robertino.

Robertino's mother and father looked at each other. They were too ashamed to meet Robertino's eyes. Then the mother took Grandfather's arm and led him back to the table in the dining room and stood near him and helped him as he ate his supper.

From that time on Grandfather never ate all alone in the kitchen again. He sat in his usual place, next to Robertino, in the dining room.

And Robertino was happy again, oh, so happy! His grandfather was loved and cared for, and as Robertino watched his parents he realized that they too were experiencing a new and wonderful happiness—for loving-kindness brings true and lasting happiness.

The Wise Judge

*M*any years ago there lived in the city of Florence a man by the name of Sir Rubaconte who was known to all for being scrupulously just. When he was made a judge, every citizen rejoiced. Sir Rubaconte had hardly been in office a month when a curious and difficult case came before him.

It concerned Bagnai, a good man but an unlucky one who seemed to have been born under an evil star. One day as he was passing over one of the bridges that join the banks of the Arno River, he saw a group of young horsemen galloping wildly toward him. Bagnai was terrified. To save himself from being trampled to death, he jumped up on the parapet of the bridge. But he slipped, and instead of landing on the bridge, the poor man fell and landed on a man who was sitting on the river bank, washing his feet. So violent was the crash of the fall that the man was instantly killed.

Thereupon the dead man's relatives raised a hue and cry and seized Bagnai and dragged him to Sir Rubaconte, demanding that the murderer of their relative pay for his crime with his life. That, they shouted, would be only simple justice.

Sadly Sir Rubaconte realized that it was not an easy matter to administer justice in this world. According to the law of Florence, he who killed a man was to be put to death. However, there was a difference between a murderer, who deliberately set out to commit a crime, and one who committed the same crime through circumstances beyond his control. But the judge could not make the relatives of the dead man see this difference. In vain did he try to convince them that poor Bagnai was innocent of any intentional wrongdoing.

The infuriated relatives only yelled louder, demanded that the letter of the law be followed, vowed that the honor of their family must be avenged. How else, they cried, could any man ever again wash his feet by the bank of a quiet river, in peace and in safety?

Sir Rubaconte was determined to save Bagnai, who stood silently there, confused by all the shouting and badly bruised by his fall. After a while, Sir Rubaconte rendered his decision. He directed that Bagnai should sit in the very place where the man had met his death. Then he asked that one of the relatives—the one who had yelled the loudest—should climb up on the bridge and that another should push him off so that he would be sure to fall directly on Bagnai, precisely as Bagnai had fallen on their unfortunate relative.

The accuser considered the height of the bridge, the cold waters of the Arno into which he might fall, and the damage to himself (here he cast a good look at the bruised and battered Bagnai). Without a word he turned and left the court, and silently his companions followed him. A cheer arose from the spectators as Bagnai gave thanks to the wise judge for saving his life.

The Thread of Life

When Giorgio was a little boy, he knew only happiness. He spent his days in a large garden, playing with his two big dogs under the watchful eye of his tall and silent English nurse. His mother loved him very dearly and so did his father, who romped with him when he came home at night.

Giorgio was a handsome child, with blond, curly hair and beautiful black eyes that smiled long before his lips did. His parents gratified his every desire: candy, toys, pretty clothes, long drives in the country in a coach drawn by two beautiful horses. The boy liked to sit with the coachman, who sometimes allowed him to hold the reins.

But one day this happy, carefree life came to an end. Giorgio was old enough now to learn how to read and to write, and a very earnest young man was engaged as his tutor. Every day Giorgio had to sit with his teacher and painstakingly try to learn his ABC's and form the letters, while the big dogs waited patiently outside the schoolroom, their noses pressed against the glass doors.

Giorgio was an obedient child, so he did what his mother told him to do, but he was no longer as happy and gay as he had been in the days when he played by the hour in the beautiful garden. Why did he now have to spend so many hours studying when before he could just play? He used to go off to a secluded nook in the garden, where all alone he would wonder about the change that had come over his life.

One day, when he was sitting there, curled up in the shade on the green grass, feeling very sad, there suddenly appeared before him a beautiful fairy, dressed in a silvery gown, with a crown of jewels in her hair. She touched his shoulder with her wand and spoke to him thus.

"I know your thoughts and your longings and have seen for a long time that you are no longer happy and gay. You would like to understand more, wouldn't you? Well, look"—she showed him a ball of thread—"this is the thread of your life. You can pull at it, and as you undo it your life will pass before you, and you will have whatever you wish. But be careful, for the end of the thread can be reached more quickly than you think, and the end of the thread will bring the end of your life. Do you understand?" She gave him the ball of thread, and saying "Farewell," she disappeared.

Giorgio sat there, astonished, bewitched by the beauty of the fairy, not understanding completely what had happened and thinking that perhaps he was dreaming. But no, he wasn't dreaming, for clutched in his hands was the ball of thread. And he had only to pull it if he wanted something.

"Giorgio! Giorgio! Where are you?" His mother's voice came to him. "Your tutor is here. It's time for your lesson."

The boy remembered what the fairy had said and thought, Suppose I pull this thread? What will happen? Will there come an end to all this studying? I'd like to find out.

So he gave the end of the thread a gentle pull and immediately felt a sudden change in his body and mind. He was no longer a child but a lad of fifteen, tall and strong and handsome. He thought no longer of his toys and of his garden. Life was beckoning. There was swimming, pretty girls with whom he danced at parties, his very own horse and hunting dogs. So time passed, and Giorgio savored every moment of this entrancing period.

One day he met his older cousins, who were studying law at the university. He

listened to them as they talked, and he yearned to be one of them. He had not thought of the thread for a long time, but now he remembered it and went upstairs to his room. He took the ball of thread out from the drawer in his desk where he kept it so carefully and pulled at it again. At the same moment he became a young man, more handsome than ever, eager to learn and to live.

He plunged headlong into his new state. He attended the university, and when he finished studying he went hunting, or to theater parties or the opera, or on long trips in his beautiful new carriage. He was so absorbed in himself and in his activities that he did not even notice his parents' hair was turning gray and that his mother was beginning to feel some of the miseries of old age.

But there came a day when Giorgio began to weary of seeking amusement. He wanted a home of his own, a lovely wife, and sweet children. It was so easy to gratify this wish. He pulled at the thread, and all of a sudden Giorgio found himself in an imposing house with spacious lawns, a beautiful wife at his side, and a rosy baby boy laughing in the cradle. It was not long before another baby boy came, and then two little girls, and then another boy. Giorgio was very happy. He loved his wife and his children, who laughed and played all day long with their little friends, bringing much joy to their parents.

On his eightieth birthday Giorgio sat all alone in his room, holding the ball of thread. What more can I want? he thought. What more can I do for my children and the little grandchildren I love so much? Nothing more? Well, then, what can I ask for myself?

There was a sound of hurrying footsteps on the stairs and happy voices calling, "Grandfather! Grandfather! Happy birthday. Happy birthday to you!"

Six laughing curly-headed children burst into the room, heaped packages on his desk, flung themselves at him, and held him close in giant hugs. Giorgio embraced each child tenderly. Suddenly he knew what he wanted for himself. He walked slowly to his desk, opened the bottom drawer, put the ball of thread—now so small, oh, so very small—into it, and locked the drawer.

Giorgio would have been content now to keep things as they were, to let his life go on without change, but one day his wife reminded him that they should think of the welfare of their children and that he must find a way to provide a bright future for them.

So Giorgio pulled at the thread again, and again he had all that he wanted: financial success, great esteem among his friends, important business connections. He was absorbed in his affairs. His help and counsel were asked on every side. Best of all, he could plan that his children need never be in want.

But as time went on, Giorgio began to feel that there was something lacking. He talked about this to his wife, who in her sweet way told him that what they needed near them were the happy voices of many grandchildren.

"Grandchildren!" cried Giorgio. "Are we ready for grandchildren? Why, it seems only yesterday that…"

He went up to his room, took out the ball of thread, and saw with sadness that not much of it remained. He recalled the words the fairy had spoken so long ago: "Be careful, for the end of the thread can be reached more quickly than you think." How truly she had spoken. Life itself was the most precious of all gifts, and he reflected with sorrow how people lose sight of this knowledge in their haste to acquire fame and fortune. "The only thing the thread cannot give is time," he said to himself, "time just to enjoy each moment without always wanting to hurry on to the next."

Nevertheless, he knew what he had to do. So once more he pulled the thread. . .

His children's wedding festivities and eventually the arrival of their delightful babies soon brightened his days and drove away his sad thoughts. He was happy again, playing with his grandchildren, watching life go on, opening like a flower before him.